MI29

of related interest

The Adventure of Maisie Voyager
Lucy Skye
ISBN 978 1 84905 287 0
eISBN 978 0 85700 604 2

Trueman Bradley – Aspie Detective
Alexei Maxim Russell
ISBN 978 1 84905 262 7
eISBN 978 0 85700 547 2

Frog's Breathtaking Speech
How Children (and Frogs) Can Use Yoga Breathing
to Deal with Anxiety, Anger and Tension
Michael Chissick
Illustrated by Sarah Peacock
ISBN 978 1 84819 091 7
eISBN 978 0 85701 074 2

Healthy Mindsets for Super Kids
A Resilience Programme for Children Aged 7–14
Stephanie Azri
Foreword by Jennifer Cartmel
Illustrated by Sid Azri
ISBN 978 1 84905 315 0
eISBN 978 0 85700 698 1

Promoting Psychological Well-Being in
Children with Acute and Chronic Illness
Melinda Edwards and Penny Titman
ISBN 978 1 84310 967 9
eISBN 978 0 85700 395 9

Extreme Parenting
Parenting Your Child with a Chronic Illness
Sharon Dempsey
Foreword by Hilton Davis
ISBN 978 1 84310 619 7
eISBN 978 1 84642 772 5

MI29

MOUSEWEB INTERNATIONAL TO THE RESCUE!

S. J. TOZER

Jessica Kingsley *Publishers*
London and Philadelphia

First published in 2014
by Jessica Kingsley Publishers
73 Collier Street
London N1 9BE, UK
and
400 Market Street, Suite 400
Philadelphia, PA 19106, USA

www.jkp.com

Library of Congress Cataloging in Publication Data
Tozer, S. J. (Sarah Jane)
    MI29 : Mouseweb International to the rescue! / S.J. Tozer.
        pages cm
    Summary: Operating out of a lost property cupboard
at Abbotsford Airport, Mouseweb International
agent Windsor Smith and his family devise a plot to help
Lily Jane Watson, a thirteen-year-old human in
desperate need.
    ISBN 978-1-84905-496-6 (alk. paper)
    [1. Spies--Fiction. 2. Brothers and sisters--Fiction. 3. Mice-
-Fiction. 4. Sick--Fiction. 5. Rats--Fiction.] I.
Title.
    PZ7.T672Mi 2014
    [E]--dc23
                                        2013030411

British Library Cataloguing in Publication Data
A CIP catalogue record for this book is available from the British Library

ISBN 978 1 84905 496 6
eISBN 978 0 85700 895 4

Printed and bound in Great Britain

For my wonderful family

MI29

BY AGENT "A"

CHAPTER 1

"Wheeeee!" shrieked India at the top of her voice. "This is fun, Sydney. What a great idea!"

The mice were speeding around the wet washbasins in a ladies' toilet at London airport. They had squeezed out some slippery liquid soap and rubbed it over their paws so that they could glide along like skaters. There was Sydney, wearing small, round glasses and a denim jacket; India, who was tall and sporting a navy-blue tracksuit; then Rio, who was wearing a football shirt with his name on the back; and not forgetting Florence, who was the youngest and smallest and was dressed up in her pink fairy outfit.

"Watch me!" cried Rio as he slid down into one basin and up the other side, bumping straight into Florence, who was spinning in front of the mirror.

"Uff!" they both gasped as they fell down in a heap.

Suddenly, they heard footsteps and voices in the corridor outside.

"Quick – someone's coming!" shouted Sydney, who was in charge, being the eldest. "Hide!"

Just in time, the mice squeezed through a vent in the wall. They peeked through the gaps to see two women enter the toilets, dressed in overalls and pushing a cart loaded with mops, brooms, cloths and cleaning sprays.

"Goodness me, Doris," said one, "it looks like there's been a flood. Children messing about again, no doubt."

"They just don't know how to behave these days, Hilda," said the other woman as she started to wipe the basins. "If I get my hands on them… Now, we must make sure to leave those *stickies* that Mr Clamp gave us today."

"Yes. Don't want to annoy the boss."

The mice hunkered down in the dark metal air duct and waited until the cleaning ladies were gone. Dusty cobwebs made them cough and sneeze, and India shuddered at the spiders and dead flies. When the door closed behind the women, Sydney beckoned his brother and sisters to climb back out of the vent.

"Come on, you guys. We'd better make sure we've covered our tracks or Mum will freak out in case they find us and then we'd have to find a new home."

"We don't want that," said Rio. "I love living in the airport."

His siblings nodded in agreement. The airport was a busy place, with so much to see and do. There was the radar aerial you could climb on that would whizz you round like a roundabout and give you an amazing view over the whole airport. The conveyer belts for the luggage reclaim were also great for a ride and the X-ray machines at security made for an interesting family photo. They loved going to the viewing platform nearby to watch the aeroplanes taxiing, taking off and landing. It was so exciting there with the roar of the engines, the smell of the fuel and the constant comings and goings of all the people and vehicles. Even at home, in lost property cupboard number three, there was plenty to do, rummaging about the many strange objects.

Yes, life in the airport was fun. Still, the mice were stuck there, and they often wished they could have adventures beyond the terminal – in the great big world beyond. Plus, the airport wasn't the safest place to live, what with airport manager Mr Clamp and his mission to wipe out rodents…

The mice were just checking for any remaining soapy paw prints on the sink when they were interrupted by a loud squeak from the ground.

"Help!"

It was Florence. Her four paws were completely stuck to a sheet of cardboard that was lying on the shiny floor.

"Help! I can't move!"

The other mice leapt down. They pushed. They pulled. They poked. But no matter how hard they tried, they just couldn't free their sister. In fact, she just became more and more stuck.

"I haven't seen one of these before," said Sydney. "It must be a new kind of trap."

"*Stickies*," Doris said.

"They must have laid sticky traps," said Rio.

India looked frightened. "What are we going to do now?"

"Dad," said Sydney. "Rio, go and get Dad."

Off Rio scampered.

Moments later, the mice heard footsteps approaching the door.

"Quick, back behind the vent!" Sydney grabbed India and off they went.

"What about me!" squeaked Florence in alarm.

But Sydney had no time to reassure his sister. For there was Hilda, gazing down at the frightened and trapped little mouse.

"Well, what have we got here then? Looks like we've finally caught something. Not a rat, though," Hilda said, poking Florence in the ribs. "Still alive too. The pest controller can soon change that. Dear me, Mr Clamp won't be pleased to hear that there are rats *and* mice around here. Ah well. At least there'll be one less rodent once the pest controller finishes with *you*, little mouse."

Hilda pulled Florence off the cardboard. The mouse squealed with pain as some of her fur was pulled off. The cleaning lady withdrew a small box from her pocket, placed the mouse inside and then walked out.

All Sydney and India could do was watch in horror as their sister disappeared. To the pest controller. To be exterminated.

CHAPTER 2

"What is it? What's happened? Where is she?"

Sydney and India had never been so happy to see their dad, Windsor. Minutes after Florence's abduction, there he was, puffing towards them through the dusty air duct in his old red tartan waistcoat and cloth cap, Rio bringing up the rear. Quickly, Sydney explained what had happened.

"What do we do now?" demanded India.

"There's no time to lose," said Windsor. "We've got to find Florence, and fast. The pest controller must work in the quarantine area. We'll try there first. I think I've got a contact there who might be able to help. Come on!"

Down the air duct ran the mice, and then out of a vent onto the main concourse of the airport. It was late evening and the place was deserted. Windsor led the way to a big computer screen and tapped it urgently.

"Right. This map says the quarantine area is between Arrivals and Departures. Follow me!"

They scurried down the main thoroughfare, past scores of shops selling everything you could possibly imagine and more.

"Look! Remote-controlled helicopters over there, Rio," shouted Sydney as they hurried ever onwards.

"Chocolate! Everywhere you look!" exclaimed India. There were piles and piles of the stuff. Large bars, small bars, buttons and drops, gift boxes, eggs, chocolate truffles, mints, toffees, fudges, caramels, raisins and nuts. The young mice slowed to take in the sight.

"Come on, keep up!" said their father. "You know the drill: leftovers only – unlike *that* lot."

Windsor pointed to one of the cafes where a number of shadowy figures were playing with the machines, laughing and shrieking hysterically. Coffee grounds were going everywhere, the juicer was overflowing, the toaster was smoking and rubbish bags had been ripped open, their contents spilling out everywhere.

"Rats," said their father gravely. "They're hooligans! Only moved in recently, and they've caused nothing but trouble ever since. Mr Clamp wants to kill them all. I'm sure he feels the same way about mice. Come along now. We must find Florence!"

On they ran until they reached the door to the quarantine area and squeezed under the gap beneath. They were greeted with a rather astonishing sight. The room was full of cages, hutches and pens with all kinds of dogs, cats, birds, reptiles, rabbits, snakes and other animals. They began to search each cage in turn, calling Florence's name. There was no answer.

"Oh!" sobbed India. "What if they've k-k-kill…"

Just then they heard a call from one of the cages furthest from the door. Rushing over, they finally found her. She looked ridiculous: sawdust was stuck to all her paws and in matted clumps in her fur. She brightened visibly when she saw them all.

"Get me out of here!" she squeaked.

"Windsor? Is that agent Windsor Smith?" said a fluffy white mouse in Florence's cage, who had very long whiskers and wore a monocle. He climbed off the exercise wheel and came to the front. "Is that really you? Is she…one of yours?"

Windsor nodded. "Hello, Whiskers. I wondered if we might find you here."

The young mice were very baffled by this conversation. They'd never heard their father use the name "Smith" before, let alone "Agent", and they had no idea who Whiskers was.

"I didn't realise. Let me help." Whiskers climbed up the metal bars at the front of the cage and slid open the fasteners. The door fell open. "It's an old trick," he said, smiling. "People just don't realise how easy it is to escape from one of these things."

Delighted, Florence leapt down to be with her family. Whiskers followed suit, and he and Windsor exchanged a special paw shake with only three fingers extended instead of the usual five.

"If you knew how to get out, why didn't you escape before?" India asked Whiskers, confused.

"Oh, unlike Florence here I wasn't captured. It's my job to hang out here. I keep an eye on the animals, so that your father and the rest of MI29 can intervene if there's a problem."

"MI29?" asked Sydney, Rio, Florence and India as one.

Windsor cleared his throat. "Right, well. Bye now, Whiskers, and thank you for your help."

"All part of the job," said Whiskers, winking.

"Yes, yes. Now come along, children. Your mother will be worried."

"Use the vent over there and once you get through to the ducting, follow the arrows in the dust on the wall marked with an 'A' for Arrivals, Windsor. You know the way from there," said Whiskers. "See you at the party!"

As they hurried back to the lost property cupboard, the mice bombarded their father with questions:

"How do you know Whiskers?"

"What party?"

"What's MI29?"

Finally, seeing that his children weren't about to give up, Windsor stopped, scratched his head thoughtfully, looked about the deserted air duct in which they were standing, sighed, cleared his throat and then whispered, "All right. I guess you're old enough now to know. My job is not, as you thought, testing cheese in the airport restaurant. I work for MI29 – the top branch of Mouseweb International. I am…*a spy*."

Rio gaped at India. India blinked at Florence. Florence *ooooo-ed* at Sydney. Sydney grinned at Rio. Their dad? A spy?

Life, it seemed, was about to get a lot more exciting. Like a pungent Cheddar, they could almost smell the adventure in the air.

CHAPTER 3

All the way back to the lost property cupboard, all through their late supper and all through getting ready for bed (it took ages to get Florence cleaned up) the little mice had fired questions at their father about MI29, until their mum, Victoria, had put her paw down and demanded that they get some sleep.

Now, it was the next morning and the children were determined to get some answers. Amid boxes of spectacles, watches, clothes, papers, umbrellas, shoes, false teeth, books, a plastic skeleton, crutches, several sets of golf clubs and skis, a wedding dress and a child's miniature sewing machine, the mice sat down to breakfast. It was a rather skimpy affair – some salad leaves and a small plastic carton of UHT milk, which Victoria had warmed on the central-heating pipes.

"I hate salad," said Rio, pushing the leaves around on his plate.

"Here. Have some ketchup with it. It might help. I'm sorry, but since Mr Clamp took over as airport manager, it's been harder to find decent leftovers," explained Windsor. "It's all kept too clean now, you see. It's the rats that are the problem. They leave such a mess behind – unlike us. They make the humans clean up even more."

"Enough about the rats!" declared Sydney. "Tell us about MI29."

Windsor looked at his wife. Victoria *tsked* but nodded.

"I'll do better than that, kids. Today, I'm going to *show* you. Today, you'll be trainee secret agents in the making…"

"Now, kids," said their mum, "you must be careful…"

But whatever warning Victoria was trying to give her children was drowned out by a clamour of excited squeaking.

◆❖◆❖◆

"*Immigration*" said the big sign on the wall of the room into which the mice were looking from their hiding spot in an air duct. All around, queues and queues of people were waiting patiently.

Windsor took out a tiny pair of binoculars from his rucksack. "Let's see," he said, focusing them.

"Where did you get those from?" asked Sydney.

"Specially made for me by Engineering a few years ago. Now, see him? Over there, waiting beside Desk Nine." They all looked at a rather shabbily dressed middle-aged man in a tweed jacket. "That's Sir Oswald Greenslade. He's one of the richest men in the world."

"How do you know that?" asked Rio.

Windsor paused for a minute, still squinting through the binoculars. "Desk Fourteen," he continued. "He's a football player from Barcelona. And see that girl over there beside Desk One? She's a gymnast from Birmingham, training for the Olympics. My organisation is trying to help her. Now, he's a minister from South Africa… She's a teacher from India… He's an important scientist… That lady's a university student from China… Aha. Here we go…"

"What?" chorused the young mice.

"See the old woman at Desk Three carrying the book of crosswords? She's eighty-three and was a spy for the human's Secret Service – for MI6, in fact. That's a branch of Military Intelligence not Mouseweb International. Only humans can join that one. She was there for years. Very high up. Still dabbles. She's got the highest security clearance. Aha! She's also a member of MI29. That's interesting. Holds a special passport. Been all around the world over the years. You watch. She'll pass straight through, no problem."

Sure enough, the woman collected her passport and walked past the immigration officer, giving him a vague smile.

"But how do you know all this?" asked India, intrigued.

"Take a look," said Windsor, passing her the binoculars. "See the computer screens? They give all the information the officers need to know to help them decide whether or not to let someone into the country."

"I want to see," said Florence, excitedly. "Give them to me!"

They all took turns to have a look at teachers with their groups of school children, accountants, plumbers, writers, actors, politicians, soldiers and lawyers. Eventually, Windsor put the binoculars back in his rucksack and led the young mice back down the duct.

"There's an arrow with a 'D' beside it. What's that pointing to?" asked Sydney.

"The 'D' stands for 'Departures'," replied his father.

Turning a corner, they saw a vague light at the end of the tunnel.

"I recognise this," said Rio. They were near the viewing platform. "Can we have a look?"

"Alright. We've got time."

They ran over to an air brick and peered through, their eyes aching with the brightness of the sunlight.

"Okay, who's that?" said Sydney suddenly. He pointed to a young girl with shoulder-length blonde hair wearing rather well-worn clothes. "Just a test!"

Windsor paused for a moment. "You *really* want to know, Sydney?"

"Yup," Sydney replied confidently. He was sure he'd got his father now.

Windsor reached into his rucksack and pulled out a tiny device that looked a bit like a camera. He rested it on a hole in the brick and waited. "Good. She turned round and I got a shot of her face."

He pressed a series of buttons. Nothing happened.

"Strange," he muttered, "it's not working." He pressed several more buttons. "Oh no, not those pesky rats again. They've got past the security software. I'll have to change my password."

He tapped away for several minutes. Finally: "At last! Well, well. Her name is Lily Jane Watson. She lives in London with her mother and father at twenty-nine Cloudesley Road, NN1. She has no brothers and sisters. She's thirteen years old and goes to Greenacres School. Her father has two jobs, and her mother works too. They're not wealthy at all. In fact, no member of her family has ever held a passport before. I would imagine she's never been on a plane. I guess that's why she comes here. To watch and wish."

There was a stunned silence.

"What on earth is that?" asked Rio, pointing to the device.

"It recognises faces," replied Windsor. "Top of the range. It's a Questor. It took us years to develop. We spied on humans developing similar gadgets, set up our own factory and scaled the design down to mouse size. I've got full access to its output because I'm an Alpha."

"An Alpha?"

"A senior agent in Mouseweb International."

"But what does it do?" said Rio.

Windsor paused. "It usually works first time, but we've had a slight technical hitch. Nothing serious. It helps me do…my job."

"And what *is* your job, Dad?" asked Sydney.

"I watch people. A bit like the people do in Immigration. We can access their information too, if we need it. We've got information about everybody! My organisation tracks people and tries to help them if they need it and deserve it."

"I think Lily looks rather sad," said Florence.

Their father looked at her. "Don't worry, dear. She's one of our branch's targets." He looked down at the screen for more information. "There are a number of reports about her here. One is prepared by an agent who lives in her house – behind the skirting in her bedroom. He's keeping a close eye on the situation." He read a bit more to himself. "It all sounds a bit grim, though…"

"Why?" asked Florence.

Windsor paused to read some more. "Not a word about this to anyone, my dears. If you want to become agents yourselves eventually, the first thing you have to be able to do is to keep secrets. Promise?"

They all nodded quickly.

"To cut a long story short, Lily isn't very well. She suffers from a rare condition and her doctors don't seem to be able to help. She doesn't have many good friends. Her teachers are unsympathetic. Hardly sees her parents because they work so hard. Cries herself to sleep at night."

India sniffed. Sydney put an arm around her and Windsor handed her a hanky from his rucksack.

"That's really sad, Dad," said Florence.

"Is there nothing we can do to help?" asked Rio.

Windsor smiled at the downcast mice. "I was hoping you'd feel this way. If you want to learn about MI29, this is the perfect mission. I have an idea that could help…"

"What are we waiting for?" said Sydney eagerly. "Let's go."

CHAPTER 4

"Urgh. This is stinky!" declared India.

"Gross. I've got GOO stuck to my paw," moaned Florence.

The mice were standing amid a sea of bins in the airport's main rubbish collection point. The bins were enormous – huge rectangular containers in various vibrant colours. They smelt terrible.

"Come on," said Windsor encouragingly. "Let's kill two birds with one stone. Here, we can stock up on food for your mother *and* help Lily."

"How is getting filthy in all this rubbish going to help Lily?" grumbled India.

"Being a secret agent isn't always glamorous," said Windsor. "It's not all like James Bond. Look, here's my idea. There's a competition on at the moment. If you find a bottle lid with a gold aeroplane drawn on the underside, you win a holiday of a lifetime. It's just what Lily and her parents need."

"So we're going to try to find one?" said Rio uncertainly, looking around at the many rubbish bags. "The chances aren't very good, are they?"

"There are quite a few winning lids out and about, I gather," said Windsor. "We know some people who have won already. There's a lot of rubbish here, so there's a chance we might find one if we all get stuck in."

"Come on," said Sydney with determination. "Let's have a go. I vote we search the yellow bin first. The one with the lid propped open."

They climbed down into the bin and started to rummage around. It wasn't a pleasant job at all. There were sticky food containers, sweet wrappers, used tissues and, worst of all, dirty nappies.

"Any luck?" asked Windsor from time to time.

"Nothing."

"Nope."

There were plenty of lids but not the right sort.

Then, "What's that noise?" said Florence.

Scurrying sounds from outside the bin had the mice twisting around to look up. But all they could see were the dirty yellow walls of the bin and, beyond, a cheery blue sky.

"Probably nothing..." Windsor began, and continued his search, but Rio interrupted him.

"There! Look! A tail! Thick, fat, wormy!"

"There's another!" shouted Sydney. "By the edge."

There was no time to state the obvious – that they had visitors in the form of rats – for the next moment the lid of the bin zoomed down and, with a thunderous crash, cut off all light.

"Trapped!" gasped Florence.

From outside came hoots and shouts and boisterous laughter. "Suckers!" shouted one.

"Those meddlesome rats," said Windsor crossly. "Now, dears, don't worry. These lids can open from the inside too, you know. I'll just climb up and..."

He was interrupted by a deafeningly loud rumbling, grumbling sound followed by an ear-splitting mechanical screech.

"The bin lorry!" Windsor shouted.

Moments later, the bin was in motion, moving up, up, up into the air, and then the lid flew open and the mice were tipped out, squealing. They landed heavily and were promptly buried by rubbish bags.

Then came the deafening noise of a motor, and the rubbish began to move, squeezing inwards. The contents of the lorry were pushed tighter and tighter around the mice. It was so dark that they couldn't see a paw in front of their faces. They panicked…

"Dad!"

"Help!"

"Ooof…can't…move…"

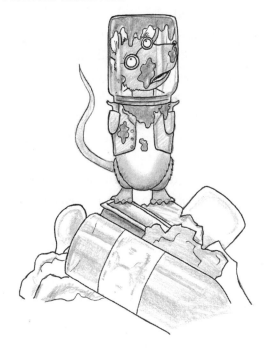

…all except Sydney, who had ended up with his head firmly lodged inside a small half-full jam jar. He gave it a lick. He had never tasted jam before and it was absolutely delicious.

Then the motor noise cut out, the crushing halted, the lorry's engine started and the mice were in motion, joggling and swinging around. It was absolutely terrifying – they could hardly breathe and the smell was awful, sickly and sweet.

After what seemed like hours but probably wasn't, the truck stopped again. Now what? They were moving again, tipping up this time. It was very disorientating. Suddenly, they felt almost weightless and then they landed with a soft thud.

Quiet descended.

One by one, the mice crawled out into the bright daylight. All around was rubbish for as far as the eye could see, blowing gently in the slight breeze.

"Are you all right?" asked Windsor.

India, Florence and Rio nodded.

"Where are we, Dad?" asked Florence.

"The council rubbish dump."

"At least there's a better chance of finding a winning lid here," said India.

Windsor, who had been muttering something about rats and cutting off tails with a carving knife, now beamed. "That's the spirit!"

They looked high and low for what seemed like hours and were just about to give up when there was a cry of victory.

"Found one!"

Florence was standing proudly atop a pile of festering rubbish, waving the lid above her head like a trophy. The gold aeroplane painted onto the inside glittered in the sun.

The others rushed over to examine the lid and congratulate Florence.

"I'll have that," said a rat suddenly appearing from nowhere. It snatched the lid from her, put it in its mouth and made off with it as quick as a flash. They were all so startled that it took a moment for them to react.

"Quick! After him! He must have been spying on us," shouted Windsor running after the rat. "Come on. Follow me!"

They ran and ran over the rubbish. It was like a very long obstacle course.

"I can't keep up. Wait for me!" cried Florence.

Just when they thought they had lost the rat, a large mechanical digger scooped up some rubbish right in front of them. The lid of the machine's bucket closed quickly as it lifted the rubbish high up into the air.

"Aaargh!" came the bloodcurdling cry from the rat as it was caught in between the digger's claws. The bottle lid dropped out of its mouth and fell down near Sydney, who raced over to pick it up.

"Well done," said Windsor.

"But how are we going to get the lid to Lily?" asked India.

"Ways and means," said Windsor mysteriously. "First, though, let's get back to the airport before any other rats can catch up with us."

He opened his rucksack, put the lid inside and took out his Questor. "Location?" he said into it urgently. He looked at the screen for a moment. "Fairview Dump, Stacksfield," he told the mice.

"Stupid name for this place," commented India.

"Gosh," said Rio. "Voice recognition? Satellite technology too?"

"Yup," said Windsor. "Tracking technology. Clever, isn't it? Everyone in MI29 has a Questor which they keep with them at all times so that all the members in the organisation know where you are at any given time."

He pressed a button on the device and spoke into it: "Dial Eddie."

Back in the lost property cupboard, the mice excitedly related their adventure to their mother. Spying on Immigration. Seeing Lily. Rooting through the rubbish. The rats' attack. Getting almost crushed to a pulp by a rubbish lorry. Finding the winning bottle lid and then almost losing it again. And their amazing journey home – in a black cab driven by Eddie, also known as Agent T, a human member of MI29, with whom Windsor chatted to using the Quester for voice amplification and translation.

Victoria listened, appalled by the danger her children had faced, furious with the villainous rats, delighted by the find of the bottle lid, but mainly horrified by the stench emanating from her family. She hustled them over to a deserted washroom and ran each sink full of hot, soapy water, then dunked them in for a thorough scrubbing.

As he wriggled under his mum's firm grasp, Sydney asked Windsor, "How many people have you helped with MI29, Dad?"

"Oh, heaps," he said. "It's all about spycraft and technology. We're all spies in our various ways. It's the way you use the information that counts. The other day, for example, I logged into the aeroplane reservation system and rearranged the seating on a plane so that a young lad who wants to be a racing car driver was sitting next to an actual racing driver…"

"So it isn't just chance who you get seated next to on a plane?" asked Rio.

"No, not always. We've even had a few humans get married after we arranged for them to meet."

"Can you do the same for buses and trains too?"

"Yup. And with tickets to all forms of entertainment – concerts, the theatre, films and sports events. Humans don't realise how much they can be manipulated now they're so dependent on computers."

"Do the public realise you can access all this stuff?" asked India.

"Only those at the very top. We came to an arrangement a few years ago. The Secret Service stopped regarding us as pests or pets and realised our potential as spies. We're inquisitive, we can squeeze through the tiniest hole and we live wherever humans live around the world."

"So how could we join MI29?" asked Sydney.

"Well…you have to do something worthwhile and be put forward by an existing member. A vote is taken, and if a majority of the agents think you're made of the right stuff, you're invited to join. You start at the lowest grade and work your way up to become an Alpha, like me."

Cogs turned in the little mice's brains. Do something worthwhile and they could be secret agents and have adventures every day… Something worthwhile – like helping Lily?

"Dad," said Sydney. "How can we get that bottle lid to Lily so she can win the holiday?"

"Ah," said Windsor. "That's simple. You wait and see."

CHAPTER 5

It was the next morning and Windsor, Sydney, Rio, India and Florence were in the air ducts on their way to Lily's house. But they had found their way barred by the rat gang.

"Well, well! If it isn't Windy, my old mate!"

The rat was wearing a heavy silver chain around his neck and carrying a black bag. He had a distinct kink in his long, thick, black tail. Behind him stood his gang – a motley lot. One had a diamond in his ear and purple fur; one had crooked, stained teeth and wore a dirty top full of holes; another had a large scar across his neck and was wearing a black vest; and the last one walked with a limp and wore a white silk scarf and a black trilby hat.

"You're no mate of mine, Hack," spat Windsor. "Why, your nasty trick yesterday might have…"

"Yeah, yeah, yeah," said Hack. "Whatever. Come on, lads. Let's not waste any more time here. Money, money, money. Time's money."

His bag was obviously full of coins and they clinked as he ran past them. There was a nasty mouldy smell surrounding them all and one of the rats trod on Sydney's tail.

"Oh, *so* sorry," he said mockingly.

The rest of the rats laughed as they scuttled past. Florence shivered as she remembered the last time she'd heard that sound – right before being trapped in the bin lorry.

"See you later, Windy," Hack taunted from behind.

"Ever get the impression we're being followed around?" muttered Windsor darkly after the rats had gone.

"Who are they?" asked India.

"Bad rats. They go around stealing. They try to help all the bad folks in the world, and to make mischief. They've got their own network all around the planet with computers and other equipment. Everything they need to get up to no good…"

"What are they doing in the duct?" asked Rio.

"I really don't know. It's the first time I've come across them there. It's…"

"What?"

"…bad news. They can now get around the airport undetected by humans. Like we can. But don't worry about it. They'll get their comeuppance one of these days. Now let's go. We've got *good* work to do while they do their bad deeds."

They ran on for some distance following arrows in the dusty walls of the air duct marked with a "B" for Baggage Reclaim. They finally came to an opening in the wall of a very large room, which was full of bags moving around on conveyor belts going in lots of different directions. This was the back end of the baggage reclaim system and there was not a person in sight.

"Jump on!" called Windsor, climbing up onto the machine. The mice followed him and watched as he started to press his Questor up against the labels stuck around the handles of the luggage.

"That thing's a scanner too," said Rio, amazed.

"I'm looking for a suitcase from NN1, preferably," said Windsor.

"What's NN1?" asked India.

"It's the part of London where Lily lives."

As the conveyor moved around, Windsor ran between each of the suitcases and examined their labels in turn. Finally, he found what he was looking for.

"This one's going near Lily's house. Climb in and enjoy the ride!" he said.

"What?" said Florence, uncertainly.

"Come on. It's the only way we're going to get to Lily's. Eddie is busy today with some other calls."

Windsor unzipped the case slightly and they scrambled in. Fortunately, it wasn't too full. He closed the zip just enough so that he could still see out.

"Here goes!"

The case tipped slightly.

"We're on a carousel now in Baggage Reclaim. We need to be patient."

Round and round they went, and they began to wonder whether their case would ever be claimed. Finally, their suitcase tipped over.

"We're on a trolley now. It belongs to a lady. Looks friendly enough. On her own, I think," Windsor whispered.

"It's a bit stinky in here," said Florence, pinching her nose.

"It's full of dirty laundry! Yuck!" said India.

Sydney snorted. "At least it's not as bad as the rubbish tip."

As they bumped along, Windsor kept them updated about where they were. They changed from the underground to a bus and then rattled down a few streets.

They were all out of the suitcase in a flash once Windsor gave the word and the young mice followed their father down the pavement, amazed at the size of the houses. It was a lovely sunny day. Not many people were around, luckily, and if someone did come along, they dived into a nearby garden to hide.

"Watch out for cats," said Windsor as he ran on ahead so fast the little mice could barely keep up. At last, he came to a halt. "Here we are," said Windsor, "Cloudesley Road. Number twenty-nine. Lily's home sweet home."

The mice looked up at the house.

"Goodness," said Sydney. "Lily does need our help…"

CHAPTER 6

The house was in a very sorry state. Paint was peeling off the door and window frames, there was a large crack in one of the walls, the garden was overgrown and one of the upper windows had a large hole in it which was covered over on the inside with some wooden boarding.

As the mice stood, gaping, there was a scrabbling noise from nearby and a small white mouse with slightly bent whiskers popped out from behind a step.

"Over here!" he beckoned.

They followed him up the steps to the front door and squeezed underneath it to get inside. They scuttled past a large pile of unopened post.

"Hello, folks! Agent Mills at your service. But you can call me Lionel. So, who are you all?"

Windsor introduced each of them in turn and the mouse shook their paws very solemnly. "Nice to meet you all," he said. "I've heard a lot about you. All good, of course. Follow me! Nobody's back yet. I'll give you a guided tour."

They followed the mouse along the hallway. The carpet was filthy.

"That's the lounge," he said, pointing at a closed door, "and that's the downstairs toilet."

They looked inside. Some of the tiles were cracked, some had fallen off completely and cups were arranged all around the toilet seat.

"That doesn't look very hygienic," said Windsor.

"Mrs Shepton, the landlady," he replied. "She washes up in the washbasin when the kitchen is full of dirty china. She's dreadful. That's why it's all in such a mess. She takes the rent and does absolutely nothing in return. She's supposed to look after Lily while her parents are working. You should see the food she cooks..." He drifted off. "Really, Lily looks after herself."

"Why don't the family move house?" asked India.

"Can't afford to," said Lionel. "Shall we go upstairs? Lily's room is in the attic. More stairs, I'm afraid."

They climbed up the dusty staircase. It was hard work but they finally reached a tiny box room. Like the rest of the house, it was absolutely freezing and there was a large patch of damp on the ceiling. There was a poster on the wall showing a map of the world, a tired and battered desk and chair, and an old-fashioned brass bed with a patchwork quilt and one saggy pillow. Propped up against that was a rather sad-looking teddy bear. Its fur was bald in places and it had only one eye.

"It's rather gloomy in here, isn't it?" said India.

They heard a noise downstairs.

"That's the front door. It's probably Mrs Shepton. She's usually home first. Come and see where I live..."

They followed Lionel under the bed and through a small hole in the wall.

"Is Lily's situation going to get worse?" asked Florence when they were sitting in his little room behind the skirting.

"We're not sure," he replied.

There was a pause as the mice looked at each other sadly.

"Does she know you're here?" asked India.

"Yes. She brings me titbits back from her school lunch, but it's really no better than the food here," replied Lionel.

"What are we going to do?" asked Florence.

"Wait till she gets back, dear," said Windsor. "We've got a plan."

They could hear pots and pans being clattered around in the sink below.

"Mrs Shepton's making dinner. I wonder what's on the menu tonight?" said Lionel. "Probably cheap sausages and packet mash with watered-down orange juice for Lily. She keeps the best food for herself. She's so mean. I've been authorised by the Alphas to make some mischief."

"What sort of mischief?" asked Florence.

"Basic stuff like moving her keys and her spectacles around so she can't find them, setting the toaster up higher so that the toast is burnt..." The front door banged shut. "That's Lily home from school."

Minutes later, Lily walked slowly into the room. The mice watched from under the bed as she sat down at her table, moved a model aeroplane to make some room and began to write.

"She loves writing. She's good at it too," said Lionel proudly. "Got an A in her last creative writing project at school."

"Now?" asked Windsor.

"As good a time as any," replied Lionel.

"What are we going to do?" asked India.

"Watch!" replied Windsor.

He and Lionel ran over to a bottle that was lying under the bed. It was full.

"How did the lid get *there*?" exclaimed Sydney. "On the drink?"

"Ways and means… Come on, help us!"

They all helped to carry the bottle and placed it on the floor beside the bed. Windsor and Lionel started to eat crumbs nearby. "Make as much noise as you can," they told the others. The mice scrabbled and scraped about.

"Hello!" said Lily, looking down from the desk. "It looks like you've brought some friends this time. I don't think I've got enough food for all of you…" She noticed the bottle. "Oh, what's that?" They watched with bated breath as she picked up the bottle and unscrewed the cap. She took a gulp. "Nice. What is it?" She looked at the label. "Pineapple and strawberry crush." She read on slowly, "*You…could…win…a…trip…of…a… lifetime. Look…for…the…aeroplane…symbol…on…the… underside…of…the…lid…*Where's it gone?" she said, rummaging around. The lid fell on the floor. "Got it!" she said. "No way! No! I've got a golden aeroplane! Wow! I usually never win anything." Lily looked down at the mice. "A free trip abroad, it says. On a plane. Do *you* know where this bottle came from?"

Then she threw her head back and laughed. "Listen to me. I'm talking to mice like I expect them to answer. I must be losing the plot. Good job I've won a holiday because I think I need one!"

CHAPTER 7

Life seemed rather dull back at the airport for the next few days, and the mice were itching for another outing. At least they had received a favourable report from Lionel: Lily had shown her mother the lid, rung the number and secured them a week's holiday anywhere in the world, travelling first class all the way.

Come Saturday night, Windsor and Victoria were preparing to go out to their party. Sydney had begged to go, but had been refused.

"It's for MI29 members only, son," said Windsor.

"Maybe one day, love," said Victoria. "Night, night. See you in the morning."

It was most frustrating, Sydney felt. After all, he was the oldest and the bravest and the wisest. But then he had a thought. What makes a secret agent? The ability to be *secretive*. So Sydney decided he would sneak out, past the babysitter, Chelsea, who came to stay with them, and do a little spying of his own.

He waited until Florence, India and Rio were asleep, and then crept out of bed and got dressed. The party was fancy dress – Windsor was dressed as Einstein and Victoria as an Egyptian princess – but all Sydney could find to wear was Florence's pink fairy dressing-up outfit, which Victoria had made for her. Good job the others wouldn't see!

Out into the airport concourse the fairy mouse scampered. A little eavesdropping had given Sydney the location of the party, and he was delighted to find the route took him on a travelator – a moving walkway. It was such fun going at speed and there were brushes at either side of the walkway, which he used to comb his fur. It struck him, as he glided along, that the airport was ever so quiet. Eerily so. No rats raiding the cafes tonight. He wondered where they were, and what they were up to. There was certainly no rat following him now.

Finally, he arrived at the party venue – the airport's first class lounge. At the door stood a mouse wearing a black tie and tuxedo, who was checking guests in against a list of names on his clipboard. As bold as brass, Sydney joined the line and waited his turn. He listened to the conversations of the excited mice in front of him.

"Did you hear, Mildred, one of the senior agents wanted to stow away on a plane to Paris, France, and ended up in Paris, Texas!"

"Funny you should say that. I know a mouse who wanted to go to Perth, Australia, and ended up in Perth, Scotland!"

"There are mice here from all over the place – from the London Underground, country mice, city mice etc. Some have flown in from all around the world, you know. I heard one has come from as far away as Timbuktu!"

The queue gradually moved forward until Sydney was just behind the front two mice in the line.

"Numbers?" asked the mouse in the tux, consulting his clipboard.

"Agent 496835 and Agent 382059," said the mice in front, who were wearing pirate costumes.

"Password?"

"Cheddar," they whispered so quietly that Sydney barely heard it.

"You're in. Next!"

Sydney moved forward.

"Number?"

Sydney said the first number that came into his head. "Agent 958404."

The mouse checked his list.

"Not on here. Where are you from?"

"I only booked at the last minute. I'm...with Windsor...Agent Windsor Smith."

"Oh. I see. Password?"

"Cheddar," whispered Sydney confidently.

"You're in. Next!"

Sydney scuttled through the door before the mouse could change his mind.

The lounge was full of all kinds of mice wearing all sorts of unusual costumes. They were dressed up as dogs, cats, bees, robins, monsters, mummies and ballerinas. There were kings and queens, cavemen, monks and nuns, clowns, nurses and doctors, cowboys and Indians, policemen and soldiers. In the distance, Sydney could just see the top of Windsor's white Einstein wig and Victoria's headdress. They were completely surrounded by other mice talking to them. In one corner, a television was on. Music was playing and some of the mice were dancing. A table in the other corner was groaning under a selection of nuts and chocolate puddings.

Sydney headed to the catering table, grabbed a chocolate éclair and stood against the wall, watching the partygoers. It wasn't long before the master of ceremonies – a rather portly, elderly mouse wearing a dress suit with a row of medals attached – called the room to attention. He was using his Questor as a megaphone.

"Ladies and gentlemen. If you'd like to gather round, we have some business to attend to before the evening's entertainment can begin."

All the mice collected under the television.

"Right. I assume you've all got your Questors? Good. Let's make a start. As you know, we need to do some case presentations regarding our future operations." He pointed his Questor up at the television and the screen jumped into life. "When they're all over, please vote in the usual way for those you think we should support."

Sydney watched, fascinated, as television footage depicted the stories of various cases MI29 was following. There was David, a ten-year-old refugee, now living in Spain, who was desperately worried about relatives who were still living in a drought stricken part of Africa. Then there was Amala, an eight-year-old orphan, who was living in a concrete pipe in the slums of Mumbai in India. All day, every day, she wandered the streets alone, begging for money for food. There was Elsie, an elderly widow living in an old people's home in Birmingham, who was terribly lonely as her nearest relatives lived a long way away. The case list was very long and, at times, heartbreaking. Just how did you choose which to vote for? wondered Sydney. He'd have liked to have helped them all.

After the voting, there was dancing and a comedy sketch show. But Sydney's favourite event was the quiz. He joined a group of mice and stayed quiet throughout, but he had fun working out the answers. Some were easy, like, "What is the name of Mickey Mouse's girlfriend?" Some were harder, like, "Who wrote *Of Mice and Men*?" He particularly enjoyed the "Name That Cheese" round, where he got to try some new and wonderful cheeses. His favourite was Jarlsberg from Norway.

After the quiz came an auction to raise money. Sydney found his paw twitching at one of the prizes – a selection of cheese from all around the world delivered to your door every week for a year – but he managed to restrain himself from bidding. After all, he had no money to offer!

It was just as the karaoke got underway – the final activity of the evening – that the unexpected happened. One minute a tubby white mouse dressed as Harry Potter was singing "I saw a mouse! Where? There on the stair! Where on the stair? Right there! A little mouse with clogs on...", the next the first class lounge was plunged into darkness.

There were gasps and groans and a couple of shrieks and an echo of "Well, I declare! Going clip-clippety-clop on the stair". Then a familiar voice called the room to order.

"Everyone stay still," commanded Windsor's voice. "I'm sure it's just a technical glitch."

Voices all over the room began whispering and murmuring.

Sydney did as he was told, but his nose was twitching. He was sitting on a chair in the corner of the room by the sound and lighting desks and now that he could not see, he found his sense of smell was heightened. And boy, could he smell something unpleasant. It smelt mouldy and off. And then, what was that noise? A chink of metal on metal. A scrabbling of claws on the floor tiles. A brushing of something warm and furry against his leg, and then something long and thick and wormlike.

All at once, Sydney realised what was happening, and though he knew he risked being discovered by his parents, at the top of his voice he shouted, "Rats! Rats! Rats!"

It was difficult for Sydney to know what happened next, given the darkness, but judging by the cacophony he heard, pandemonium had broken out. Then, near to him, a small light appeared in the gloom – then another and another. The mice had lit up their Questors like torches, and were searching the room. With this low light in the room, Sydney could just make out cables beside him on the floor that had been chewed through. But there was no sign of the rats.

"Windsor, the power cables!"

Sydney spun around at the sound of his mother's voice. She was close. Time to go!

In all the chaos, it was easy to slip out. He hurried home, keeping a beady eye out for rats, knowing he had better get back into bed before his parents got there. Having seen all the other secret agents that evening, he knew now this was what he wanted to do with his life. And it wouldn't do at all to be discovered, on his first solo secret mission, creeping about the airport wearing fairy wings and a tiara…

CHAPTER 8

The next morning Windsor and Victoria said nothing of their brush with the rats the night before. Sydney watched them closely for any sign that either of his parents had recognised his voice warning them of the rats in the darkness of the party, but they seemed determined to focus on Lily today.

"You might be interested to know that I was talking to Lionel at the party last night, Sydney," said Windsor over breakfast. "MI29 technicians did some searches and found out that there's a doctor working in a hospital in America – in Florida actually – doing some amazing new research into Lily's illness.

"All we have to do now is get her to visit for some scans."

"Should they take their holiday in Florida, then?" asked Florence.

"Yes, I think so."

"It's an interesting place to visit, anyway," added Victoria.

"But how are you going to persuade Lily's parents to go there?"

"I talked about it last night with some of the other agents and we've made a plan. We know a mouse called Georgia, who lives in the hospital in Orlando. She's going to write an article about the work they do there and send it to Mike, our agent who works at *The Herald* newspaper."

"What's he going to do with it?" asked India.

"He's going to slip the text into the paper just before they do the print run."

"How's that going to help?" asked Florence.

"According to Lionel, Lily's father reads *The Herald* thoroughly every day, so he's bound to spot the article. It will ask people with the illness to come forward to try out a new experimental treatment."

"Wow! Do you think it's going to work?" asked India.

"We can but try," replied their father. "We did a similar thing with a speech the Prime Minister was giving at a foreign summit. We swapped the text over at the last minute. It went down very well, too. We removed all the boring stuff about economics and concentrated on increasing the charity work done by the government."

Just then they heard the door to the cupboard being opened.

"Hunt, Archie. Hunt!" boomed an unfamiliar male voice.

The mice heard the pitter-patter of feet skittering on the lino floor and scrabbling in the far corner of the cupboard.

"Quick! Through the vent!" shouted Windsor.

They all scrambled through to the other side as fast as they could, and then bunched up to watch the cupboard through the slits in the vent.

"He's coming this way. It's a Jack Russell terrier! They can be trained to hunt for rats."

A large, wet nose sniffed the vent and a loud bark made the mouse family jump.

"What, Archie? What?" said the dog's handler, urgently.

It barked again. They heard footsteps coming over towards the back of the cupboard and boxes being slid out of the way.

"What is it?" he said again.

They could see the dog sniffing around where they had eaten breakfast.

"Shhh!" said Victoria, seeing the dog cock his head to one side. It barked again.

They watched in trepidation, wondering what would happen next.

The dog sniffed Florence's bag of wool bed and then went over to some empty milk cartons lying on the floor.

"Strange…" said the man. "What are they doing there? And all these crumbs too. I must tell the cleaners to clear this up. Good boy, Archie. I'll put another trap down in the meantime just in case."

The dog sniffed around the rest of the cupboard and, finding nothing, the man said, "Come on! Let's go."

The door closed firmly behind them.

"Phew! That was close," said Rio.

"Mr Clamp's job must be on the line if they're going to these lengths to catch rodents," said Windsor.

"What are we going to do?" asked Florence.

"Lie low for a while. Retrieve what we can from the cupboard and stay behind the walls. It's the safest place. And we should definitely go away with Lily to keep an eye on her. You never know what the rats could get up to."

Sydney and his siblings looked at each other with big grins. A plane trip! A holiday! Adventure!

CHAPTER 9

For the next few days, the mice watched Hilda and Doris, the cleaners, do a complete spring clean of the lost property cupboard. Every box was sorted through and a lot of the belongings that had been there for years were finally thrown out. All of the things that had made the back of the cupboard home for the mice were put away.

"Don't worry, dear," said Windsor to Victoria, who was very upset. "We can start again somewhere new, if we have to."

It was cold, dusty, draughty and cheerless living behind the vent and the mice got hungrier and hungrier because there wasn't much in the way of food to come by around the airport. Windsor hardly dared to venture out, as the cleaners were now even searching the ducting with torches. The cafes and restaurants were being kept spotlessly clean and the food sacks outside the airport, which had yielded such a good hoard of leftovers previously, were now put in huge wheelie bins with heavy lids, which were impossible to get inside, and collected on a daily basis. Their living conditions eventually got so bad that Windsor decided the best place for them to be was at Lily's house.

When they got to Lily's, thanks to a lift from Eddie the cab driver, they were amazed to see how the house had been transformed. It had been completely repainted, the broken window had been repaired and the garden was now immaculate. Two large pot plants stood either side of the front door.

"Wow, this place has changed," said Windsor to Lionel once they were inside. "It's so clean and tidy. What happened?"

"A makeover team visited, organised by MI29," explained Lionel. "All sorts of tradesmen turned up one day and fixed up the house. For free! And now the landlady's turned over a new leaf. She was shamed into doing so, I think. She's changed – much friendlier to Lily and the family now."

"And how's Lily?" asked India.

"So excited at the prospect of the holiday. She packed a week ago!" said Lionel.

The mice climbed the stairs up to Lily's room and found that it had also been completely transformed. Instead of bare floorboards there was new wall-to-wall carpet that made it feel very cosy. The damp patch had gone and the walls had been completely redecorated with lovely light-pink paint. Some new pictures had been put up and pretty flowery curtains hung at the windows. To one side was a bookcase full of new books to read and a nice old wooden chest to keep her toys in. The old brass bed had been replaced with a brand new canopied bed made up with a thick duvet and two plump pillows. The bed was heaving with cuddly toys. The window had been double glazed to rid the room of draughts and there was a new radiator on the wall near her desk.

"Central heating?" asked Victoria.

"Throughout," replied Lionel.

"They've done a fantastic job!" said Windsor. "And all in the space of…what…ten days? Incredible."

"We had twenty-three people working here at the peak."

They heard the front door slam shut.

"That'll be Lily back from school with her mother. What's the plan, Windsor?"

"Let's wait behind the skirting until she goes to bed. We'll do the reveal then."

"The what?" asked Sydney.

"The reveal – show her that we're all back and persuade her to take us with her on the trip."

"What if she doesn't want to?" asked Florence.

"We'll stow away with her somehow. We need to keep an eye on her. I think the rats may have twigged that she's one of our special targets. Anyway, got any food, Lionel? We're all starving!"

"I thought you might be, so I stocked up. Come and see!"

Lionel had excelled himself. His little room was groaning with food. Among other things there were delicious buttered cheese scones, cheese straws, cheese and onion crisps, chocolate chip flapjacks and chocolate caramel shortbread.

"Eddie helped me by going shopping at the supermarket."

"But how did you get all of this up here?" asked India.

"Good question! I'll just say that Eddie's been well trained and is an expert in covert entry techniques."

"Picking locks without a key to open them?" asked Sydney.

"Erm…well…yes, but only with permission from the Alphas, though."

"So that's how the drink with the winning lid got up to Lily's room! He brought it up when everyone was out – just like the food," said Rio.

Lionel nodded.

There was silence as the mice tucked into the food.

"So have you ever been abroad before?" Florence asked her father a little later.

"Before you were born, your mother and I travelled a lot. We named you all after our favourite places."

Suddenly, they heard footsteps coming up the stairs.

"She's coming!"

They watched as Lily checked through her suitcase.

"Okay now, let's go."

"I'll stay here," said Lionel.

Windsor ushered his family along and they ran out from under the bed and crossed the room to where Lily was.

"Follow me!" said Sydney as he climbed up inside her suitcase.

"Are you sure about this?" said Victoria, doubtfully.

"Come on, Victoria," said Windsor. "Sydney has the right idea."

Lily soon noticed the mice in her case.

"Oh, it's you again," she said, laughing. "What are you all doing here?" Lily watched as the mice scrabbled underneath a T-shirt. "You want to come along too, do you? Well, I'm not sure what my parents would say."

Windsor took his Questor out of his rucksack and said slowly into it, "They don't have to know."

Lily froze. She blinked a few times, and then gave a shaky laugh.

"Crazy girl needs a holiday. Talking mice indeed."

"Not crazy, Lily," said Windsor. "But a holiday sounds good."

Lily's jaw dropped and she slumped down onto the bed.

"You're...but you...how can you...no way..."

Windsor was getting a little impatient. "Oh yes. This device translates and amplifies so you can hear me talk. Now then..."

But Lily wasn't about to let go of her confusion and disbelief, and it took Windsor a good ten minutes more to explain the Questor and assure her of the fact that, yes, she was talking to a mouse and, no, she wasn't crazy.

"Well, I suppose it's just one of many strange things that have happened recently," said Lily finally. "I won a holiday because this winning bottle lid just appeared and then these people arrived out of the blue wanting to tidy things up..."

"Mmm," said Windsor thoughtfully.

"Hang on. This MI29 business… This good luck I've been having isn't anything to do with you lot, is it?"

Sydney and his siblings gave excited squeaks that were answer enough for Lily.

"Wow!"

"We'd like to see our mission through, Lily," began Windsor.

But he didn't need to explain – Lily was on the case.

"Come with me! To Florida! It's thanks to you I'm going, and you can travel in my school bag, which I'm taking as hand luggage. It will be great to have some friendly faces along. I have to go to a hospital out there, you see…"

"Bedtime, Lily!" called her mother from downstairs. "Come on, we've got to get up early tomorrow to get to the airport."

"The same goes for you little mice," said Victoria sternly. "Tomorrow's going to be a big day."

"The *best* day," said Lily, eyes shining.

CHAPTER 10

"Champagne, anyone?" asked the air hostess. "And a glass of freshly squeezed juice for the young lady?"

First class! Sydney couldn't believe it. Neither could Lily and her parents. The seats on the plane were huge and spacious – lots of room for Lily's bag to sit comfortably beside her, giving the mice the chance to look about.

They had Windsor to thank for the luxurious surroundings. On arrival at the airport for check-in, he had checked his Quester and found that Lily and her parents had been seated at the back of the plane in the seats with the least leg room, surrounded by families with noisy young babies. "Those pesky rats!" he'd declared. A few clicks later, he'd swapped the booking back to first class.

Now, the plane filled up and before they knew it, they were waiting at the end of the runway to take off. The engines roared and the aeroplane started to gain speed, slowly at first and then ever faster. They were pushed back into their seats with the force of it all, and in the bag the mice clutched at each other. The aircraft tilted and the airport receded behind them. Sydney peeked up over the top of the bag and out of the window. The clouds looked like puffs of cotton wool.

"We're up!" said Lily's dad.

"Happy holiday, Lily," said her mother.

Once they were cruising, a series of wonderful meals were served up on bone-china plates and Lily fed the mice as many scraps as she could without being seen. To stretch their legs, the mice ran up and down the aircraft under the passengers' seats and, on a couple of occasions, hitched a ride on the hostess trolley as it went up and down the plane serving meals and drinks. They even managed to sneak in a quick visit to the cockpit and were amazed at the sheer number of buttons and dials the pilot had to deal with. They were so excited that the nine-hour flight seemed to pass in a flash.

After a remarkably smooth landing, they passed through the airport quickly and took a cab to the hotel. Their suite at the hotel was amazing.

"A week of luxury. How *will* we cope?" said Lily's mother, laughing as she jumped onto the enormous bed.

"My room's got a TV and its own bathroom," said Lily, wide-eyed with amazement. "It's huge! And look at the view!" She lifted up her school bag to let the mice see through the window.

"Wow!" exclaimed the mice family almost in unison.

"That's amazing," whispered Sydney through the Questor.

The family spent the rest of the day by the pool, but the next day they were ready to explore. They went to a nearby theme park. There were so many different rides it was difficult to choose which one to go on first. There were carousels, rollercoasters, water slides, corkscrew rides, big wheels, waltzers, dodgems – the list was endless. Lily's enthusiasm was endless too. She wanted to go on every ride. The mice were grateful when it was time for the big parade at the end of the day as they were starting to feel pretty sick. They had been flung around without really being able to see where they were going inside the bag and it was all very disorientating.

Over the next few days, the family went to the film studios theme park and the zoo. They tried golf, water-skiing, snorkelling, swimming with dolphins, exotic shell collecting and surfing, and took a trip on a glass-bottomed boat to see a coral reef. They also went to the Kennedy Space Centre, and after seeing the astronaut training areas, the space rockets and the launch pad, Sydney vowed that he would take a trip into space when he was older.

Then came the day they were all waiting for: Lily's appointment at the hospital. The doctor checked her over and then sent her for a number of scans. After a long wait, they were finally called in for the results.

"Well, Lily," said the doctor, "we can see your problem on the scans and...well...it's treatable. You need to try this new medicine and come back after six months. We'll review you then and take it from there. Have you got any questions?"

"Will I need an operation?"

"We'll see how things develop over the next few months. Don't worry about it. We'll cross that bridge if we come to it. Just enjoy the rest of your trip. Where are you going tomorrow?"

"The Everglades," said her father.

"Ah, off to see the alligators, are we? Have fun!"

Later that night, when Lily was in bed sleeping, the mice overheard her parents' conversation in the room next door.

"How are we ever going to be able to afford to come over here again in six months' time?"

"I don't know. The medicine isn't cheap either..."

"And I don't think I can do any more overtime than I already am."

"We'll think about it when we get back. Let's enjoy the rest of the holiday while we can."

"What are they going to do?" asked India.

"I've got an idea," said Windsor. "And, like my best ideas, it will kill two birds with one stone."

Sydney gulped. Last time Windsor had had an idea like that, the mice had nearly been squished to smithereens in a rubbish lorry...

CHAPTER 11

The next morning, their last full day of the holiday, the family rose and had breakfast in a typical American diner. They had a huge portion of eggs "over easy", bacon, sausages and hash browns. A chocolate muffin finished off the biggest breakfast Lily had ever eaten.

"This chocolate tastes different from the chocolate back home," said Florence, eating the crumbs that Lily had put in her bag.

"Mmm," they all agreed.

It was a lovely sunny day and Lily's father put the top down on the car they had hired for the day. As they sped along the highway, they passed a sign warning of alligators ahead and knew they must be getting close.

A little further on, a large sign advertising airboat trips came into view.

"Here we are," said Lily's father, parking the car. "Kissimmee."

"With pleasure!" said Lily's mother, giving him a peck on the cheek.

"No, you nincompoop idiot, that's the name of the river!"

They all laughed.

The boat they were going to take a trip on was not called an airboat for nothing. It turned out to be a large flat-bottomed speedboat with a big fan on the back to propel them along. There were several rows of elevated seats and Lily and her parents were lucky enough to get places in the front row. Lily sat at the side of the boat with her bag on her lap so that the mice could see where they were going.

When everyone was on board, the driver took his seat high up at the back and they were off. Once it got going, the noise of the engine and fan was very loud, and as they swept down the network of boggy creeks, canals, grassy rivers, marshes and swamps they could only just hear the driver as he pointed out various types of wildlife. There were large clumps of pretty waterlilies, exotic plants and trees as well as wading birds, land birds and birds of prey. They even saw a couple of turtles basking in the sun, and although they didn't see any, there were apparently snakes around too.

"Look over there!" shouted the driver, pointing to what looked like a floating log in the water some distance away. "It's a 'gator. I reckon it's over twelve feet long. The biggest they found here was over nineteen feet. Let's try to get a bit closer." The passengers all craned their necks to see the creature.

"Aargh!" shouted Lily suddenly, standing up. "A rat! It tried to crawl up my leg!" Her bag dropped like a lead weight and the mice inside were winded as they hit the deck. The mice saw a flash of black tail running towards the back of the boat. Suddenly the airboat swerved. Lily over-balanced and fell over the side with a huge splash. "Help me! Please! The alligators!" she spluttered as she came up for air.

The pilot reacted instantly and threw a floating ring with a rope attached into the water. Lily wriggled it over her head and arms so that it supported her around her waist.

"Oh my goodness!" said her mother. "We've got you Lily. Hold on tight, Quick pull her back on board!"

"Yep. I've got you," shouted the pilot. "Now don't panic!"

"It's not the rats again is it?" said Victoria, struggling to catch her breath.

"Quick! To the back of the boat!" shouted Windsor to the mice. "They won't see us as everyone is watching Lily. I think we've got company."

They followed him under all of the seats past a rather bedraggled Lily who had been hauled back onto the boat.

"It's Hack!" shouted Windsor, picking up one of a number of twigs that had dropped into the boat. "I'd recognise him anywhere. Corner him! Grab one of those twigs. Come on!" The mice circled around the rat, pointing their sticks towards him so that the fan was behind him and the water was in front.

"Now, Hack," shouted Windsor, "what are you going to do? Either the fan will chop you into tiny pieces, or are you going to take your chance with the alligators? We won't be throwing you a ring."

Hack laughed menacingly. "There are plenty more of us where I come from," he snarled, "and they can track you down just like I did. Those Questors of yours are good, but they're not quite good enough. You see... now we know how to trace them."

"Ah, that explains a lot. I thought you lot had been following us around. Forwards!" shouted Windsor. The young mice bravely advanced on the rat, who was now teetering on the edge of the boat. Suddenly, the boat accelerated and the rat tipped over the edge, shouting defiantly as he fell into the water with a big splash.

"Goodbye and good riddance!" shouted Windsor after him.

"Do you think the alligators will get him?" asked Florence.

"I don't know. Rats can swim very well..." His voice drifted off for a second or two. "Anyway well done, everyone! I couldn't have done it without you all. But there's no time for celebrations. If the rats have learnt how to trace us by the Questors, that means they've hacked into our computer system. We must hurry. The very future of MI29 is in jeopardy."

CHAPTER 12

Mouseweb Systems Control, Florida said the sign on the door.

"Not much of an HQ for MI29," said Florence, turning up her nose.

It was true that the surroundings were not exactly grand. On arriving back at the hotel Windsor hurried them all down, down, down into the ventilation ducts of the hotel to the sewers beneath, and then through a bewildering array of stinky tunnels. Several times the young mice had questioned the route, but each time Windsor told them to trust the Questor, whose map function was guiding them.

Finally, they had reached a small door in a grimy wall whose sign signalled that they had reached their destination. Windsor held his Questor up to an electronic pad set in the wall and pressed a button and the door slid open. The mice went through and, to their amazement, they found themselves in a vast, light, modern room full of small tables, chairs and computers as far as the eye could see. On the wall was a large map of the world with a network of dots on it. Some were green but others were flashing red. Mice were tapping furiously away and the room was buzzing with conversation and activity.

"Windsor!" boomed a voice, and an elderly but sprightly grey mouse sprang across the room to greet them. "Chad Murray. I got your message. We've been working hard to see how far into the computer system they've infiltrated. What's the status, Adelaide?" he asked a small black mouse who was working nearby.

"There is unfamiliar activity in networks C23 and J4. Asia is in trouble and we're waiting to see what happens to Africa."

"They've penetrated the firewalls, then?"

"Yup. We've lost three mainframes so far…"

"What about our other defences?"

"We can deploy some viruses once the backups are in place. We're working on that right now… Do we have your authorisation to go ahead, Windsor?" asked Chad.

Sydney blinked. Even here, in America, Windsor had authority? He must be a really respected Alpha.

"It would take too long to get hold of all the Alphas. I'll get on to the COMADOR emergency committee right now," said Windsor.

The young mice could only watch as he sat in front of a computer console and tapped away frantically.

"Is everything going to be alright?" Florence asked Victoria.

"We can but live in hope," she replied.

More and more of the lights started to flash red on the world map.

"We've lost Sector Nine," shouted one of the mice at the far side of the room.

"That's Central America," muttered Adelaide.

"Okay… Right… That's it. COMADOR have given the go-ahead for the viruses," shouted Windsor to all those in the room. "Stand by your work stations. Fire NONA33."

"NONA33 activated," someone called.

"What does that do?" asked Rio.

"It infects files on a network file system that's accessed by other computers. It causes files to replicate extremely quickly and chokes the server memory," replied Windsor. "Any reports of collateral damage?"

"None as yet. They haven't got into our bank accounts."

"We're picking up reports of damage to the rats' main data storage facility on the communications link," said Victoria, who was watching her Questor.

"Okay, give them all we've got," said Windsor. "Activate ALBION5."

"What's that?"

"It's our most sophisticated virus to date. It infects any computer on a specific network; causes the fan inside it to spin so fast that it breaks and the machine then overheats. Its brilliant!" said Adelaide.

"ALBION5 deployed," shouted Chad.

The whole room waited with bated breath.

"Sector Nine partially restored."

Gradually, the lights on the map started to change back to green.

"Have we got them?" asked Windsor.

"Looks a bit like it," said Adelaide.

"COMADOR are saying that the rats have lost all network coverage," said Victoria.

A cheer went up all around the room.

"That'll give them something to think about," said Windsor.

"Mainframes rebooting... Mainframes up."

The final red lights on the wall map changed to green.

"Well done, everyone!" shouted Windsor. "That was a job well done!"

"Amazing!" said Sydney to his father.

"So, are your children budding agents Windsor?" asked Chad.

"I'm training them up," Windsor replied. "There will certainly come a time when I'll need to retire – particularly if we have many more days like today. Now, I think we'll be off, if you don't mind. You've got the situation under control."

"Is it all over now, Dad?" asked Rio as the family made their way back out into the sewers.

"Dear me, no. The battle may be won, but the war rages on. There is still much to do to protect MI29's good work from the rats. That is why you all need to train hard to qualify as agents yourself. Thwarting the rats is all in a day's work for an agent," said Windsor. Then he leaned over and whispered in Sydney's ear, "As you know yourself, from when you warned us during the party blackout of the rats in the room."

Sydney gaped at his father.

Windsor grinned. "Good work, son."

"Can we join MI29 as junior agents now?" asked Sydney timidly.

"You'll have to wait for the vote. I'll certainly be putting you all forward," replied Windsor. The mice cheered and whooped – they were so happy to hear this news. "Now, we need to go back to the hotel. We've one last problem to solve today, and it's a Lily-shaped one."

Back at the hotel, the mice watched as Lily packed her case for the journey home the following day.

"Have you had a good holiday, Lily?" asked Windsor.

"The best ever!"

"You really did see a rat in the boat, didn't you?"

Lily nodded. "It tried to run up my leg. It was so scary in the water. I could have been eaten!"

"Well, that was Hack. He was trouble with a capital T. He tried to hurt you."

"Tell her the story Windsor," said Victoria. "Tell her everything, so she knows what we've been up against."

Lily listened as he explained how MI29 had been battling the rats for years.

"But that's terrible," said Lily once he'd finished, "and now you're homeless."

"But you can help us, though."

"How?"

"Let us stay with you. We'll help you write the whole story down. Change some of the names and details to protect identities, and then we know some publishers who can print it. Some of the money from the books can help pay for your treatment and the rest can go towards MI29. You help us and we can help you…"

"Okay! Let's do it!" said Lily enthusiastically.

"All for one and one for all, as they say," said Windsor. "You can be our Agent 'A', the 'author'."

"One for all and all for one," she replied. "I'll start writing the book as soon as I get back home."

So that, dear reader, is how you come to be reading this very story.

And if you happen to see a tiny mouse nearby, consider this – who is spying on who?

THE END

ACKNOWLEDGEMENTS

I would particularly like to thank my wonderful husband John for all his love, support, patience and encouragement over the years and especially during the writing process. Thanks also to my amazing mother Jeanne for being by my side every step of the way and for all her help and sound advice. To my father David goes a big thank you for my education, which has given me the opportunity to try many different things, and for encouraging me to set myself high standards. My children Kate and Nicholas deserve thanks for just being amazing and for their forthright but usually helpful comments on the manuscript. I would also like to thank my friends for their support. Finally, thanks go to Charlie Wilson at The Book Specialist Ltd for her help editing the book.